# Fancy NANCY

## Oodles of Kittens

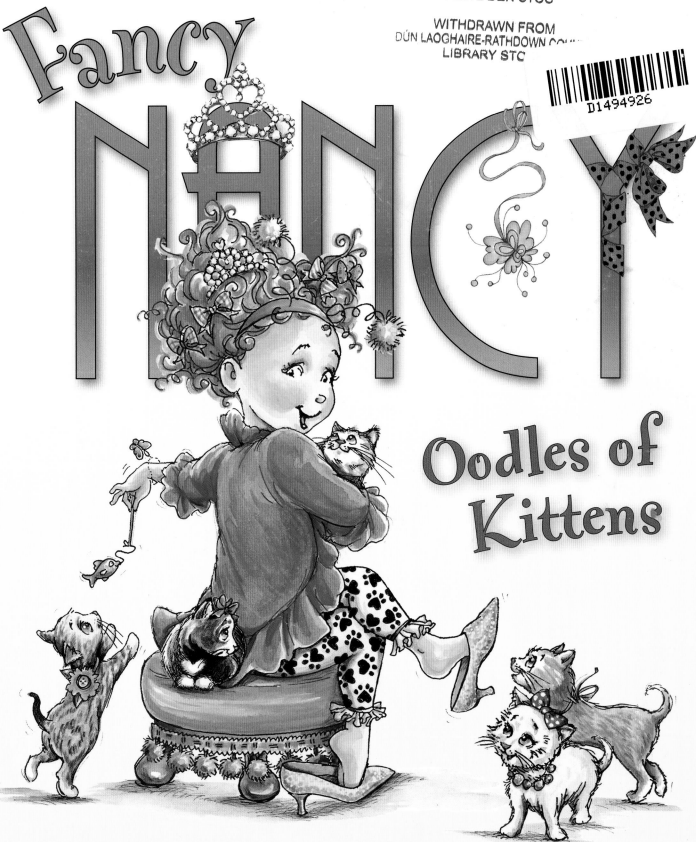

Written by Jane O'Connor · Illustrated by Robin Preiss Glasser

HarperCollins *Children's Books*

Well, we've come full circle, and I treasure every one of those 360 degrees.
Merci, merci, merci!
Love,
Jane

For Jane O'Connor, Margaret Anastas, and Jeanne Hogle,
with oodles of thanks for the gift of Nancy. xxx
—R. P. G.

First published in hardback in the USA by HarperCollins Publishers in 2018
This edition first published in paperback in Great Britain by HarperCollins Children's Books in 2018

HarperCollins Children's Books is a division of HarperCollins Publishers Ltd.

13 5 7 9 10 8 6 4 2

ISBN: 978-0-00-756094-3

Text copyright © Jane O'Connor 2018
Illustrations copyright © Robin Preiss Glasser 2018

Typography by Jean L. Hogle
Visit our website at: www.harpercollins.co.uk
Printed in China

Oh, what a dismal day! That means it's grey, grey, grey — the plainest color on earth. So we are cheering ourselves up with a tea party — Mrs DeVine, Bree, and me.

As Bree and I split the last pastry, suddenly we hear crying.

It's coming from outside.
*Eee-yewww! Ee-yewww!*

Lickety-split, we throw on our raincoats and go investigate. (That's fancy for finding out what's up.)

Lo and behold! What do we discover in the dog house?

A cat... and that's not all!

There are kittens – oodles of them!
One, two, three, four, five!

Bree and I clutch each other.
I am practically hyperventilating.
That means I'm so excited
I almost faint.

Mrs DeVine helps us get the
cat and kittens inside. "Poor
cat! She's a stray," she says. "She's
never had a home."

Then Mrs DeVine explains
that a brand-new mother cat
is called a queen.

Ooh la la! How fancy!

We find a box and line it with soft towels.

We decorate the box, and voilá – a home fit for a queen!

For many days, all we do is peek in on the little family.

The kittens cannot see or hear yet. They just sleep and drink milk.

We call the queen "Your Majesty" – "Maj" for short.

She is very nurturing, which means she is an excellent mother.

Little by little,
the kittens grow...

and change.

They are way cuter than cute.

They are precious, darling, absolutely adorable!

These two are always together. They like to roughhouse and tumble over each other. We don't like to play favourites, but I must confess we love them the best.

Mrs DeVine is going to keep Maj.
But soon it is time to find good homes for the kittens.

One by one, the kittens leave for new homes.
"Au revoir," we say each time one leaves.
That's French for "goodbye."

We are sad, but not brokenhearted, because Bree and I get to keep our favourites! We name them Sequin and Rhinestone.

I shower Sequin with oodles of attention.
I can't stop hugging and kissing her.

"No, Frenchy, I can't walk you now," I say. "It's time for Sequin's dinner." I wish I could make Frenchy understand. Taking care of a kitten is a full-time job.

Every day, Sequin and Rhinestone play together.
And if our kittens ever feel homesick for their
mother, we bring them next door. Can you think of
a more ideal arrangement?

Well, it would be ideal, except for one problem...

# Frenchy!

She doesn't like Sequin. She growls and barks at her.
"What's wrong with Frenchy?" I ask my parents.

"Maybe Frenchy is jealous," my dad says.
"She sees you giving Sequin so much attention."

"You don't remember," my mum says, "but after JoJo was born, you were very jealous."

Me? Jealous? I find that incredible. But maybe my parents are right about Frenchy.

So I shower Frenchy with oodles of attention.

I give her bubble baths.

I dress her in new ensembles.

I even let her lick peanut butter off my face.

Little by little, I let Frenchy come near Sequin.

"Sequin is only a baby. She is not mature like you," I tell Frenchy.

Then I explain that mature is a fancy word for grown-up.

Ooh la la! It seems to be working!
Frenchy stops growling at Sequin.
Soon she doesn't mind Sequin
playing with her toys.

She even lets Sequin share her doggy bed.

It is almost like Frenchy is Sequin's big sister.
It is an ideal arrangement until…

...one evening, I can't find Sequin anywhere.

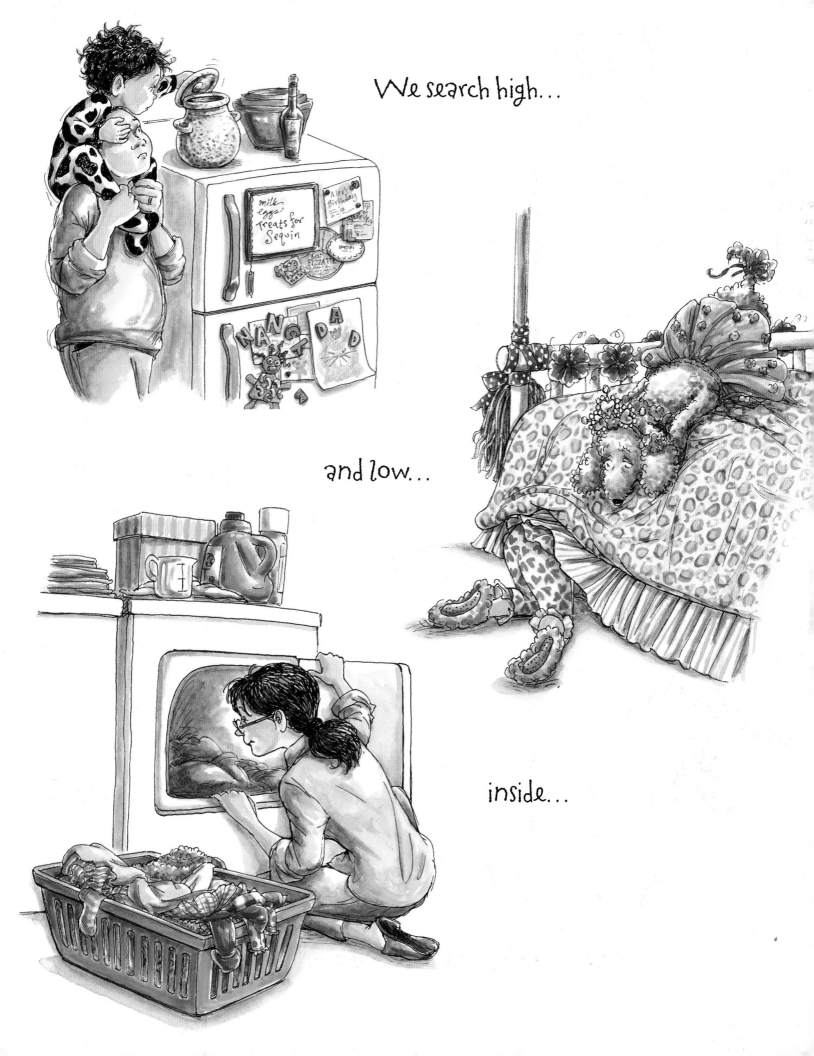

We search high...

and low...

inside...

...and outside. But it is
so dark. It's hard to see.

I am growing more and more frantic, which is fancy
for scared. What if we don't find Sequin?

Then, suddenly, Frenchy stands very still. Her ears prick up. Does she hear something we don't? Her nose twitches. Does she smell something we don't?

Lickety-split, Frenchy takes off towards the clubhouse. We all follow and – lo and behold! – there is Sequin!

I nearly faint with relief. "Merci, merci!"
I say to Frenchy.

At bedtime, we cuddle in bed.

"I love you oodles and oodles," I tell Frenchy.
"I love you oodles and oodles, too," I tell Sequin.
And though they can't talk, I know they love me
oodles and oodles right back!